THE LAST, THE LOST, AND THE LEAST

A novella based on a true story

COPYRIGHT HOLDER:

Lawrence L. Allen
DALLAS, TEXAS, USA

www.7bridgestorecovery.org

Author:

www.hangneckridge.com/the_last_the_lost_and_the_least

Publisher: Lawrence L. Allen, Dallas, Texas, USA

Cover Design by Deborra J. Dodson

ISBN: 978-0-9915826-5-5

DEDICATION

To the last, lost and least among us,

those who cannot help themselves:

there is someone that cares.

And to the author that believed

and saw the difference in a Christian

at work for all the right reasons.

ACKNOWLEDGEMENT

"Real religion, the kind that passes muster before God, is this:

Reach out to the homeless and loveless in their plight,

and guard against corruption in the Godless world."

— James 1:27

FOREWORD

A New Day Upon Us

— by Dan Wells

This is the beginning of a new day.

We have been given this day to use as we will.

We can waste it, or use it for good.

What we do today is important,

because we are exchanging a day of our life for it.

When tomorrow comes that day will be gone forever,

leaving in its place whatever we have traded for it.

We should pledge to ourselves that it "shall be:"

gain, not loss, good, not evil, success, not failure.

In order that we shall not regret the price we paid for this day.

So take this day in the beginning, with the end in mind.

CHAPTER 1

Pastor 7 hunted 'n pecked his way around his desktop computer keyboard until he'd completed the application for title transfer on the Georgia State DMV's website. After living nearly a year at Pastor 7's *The Garden* sanctuary for the last, lost and least from the streets of Atlanta, one of the residents was ready to take her next step away from despair and dependency toward redemption and independence. He was transferring into her name the title of a 1997 Chevy Malibu—recently donated to his 7 Bridges To Recovery mission. Just a day earlier, she'd received her driver's license that she'd need to get to and from the job that Pastor 7 had helped arrange for her. The car had a fresh set of tires and parolees, from one of Pastor 7's houses for men recovering from a life of addiction and crime, had just refurbished its brakes. It was ready to go another 25,000 miles. She did not know that he was doing this, and he would surprise her by handing her the keys once the title change paperwork came through in three to five business days.

One down, endless more to go. Time for an espresso.

Pastor 7 creaked his way across the century-old floor of the pastor's residence that adjoined the old church that was having a graffiti-style mural honoring the ministry painted on its side. The residence's modern refurbished kitchen was linked to an original fireplace, ensconced within plaster walls adorned with memorabilia from the church's history, by rough-hewn wooden ceiling cross beams.

Stirring sugar into his espresso before returning to his desk, Pastor 7 watched through the window as women filed between the church's old recreation center that he'd converted into a dormitory and The Garden's cafeteria where they ate three times a day. Volunteers from the Formosan Christian Church of Dallas youth group, who'd just spent their last night camping in sleeping bags on the church's floor, were serving breakfast that morning. Everything was running like a top.

A knock at the residence door brought Pastor 7 to a middle-aged woman dressed in a 1980s-style power suit. She was admiring his Harley Davidson motorcycle that was parked just outside. "Is that a 2010 Road King?"

"2007."

"David Welsh?" she turned and looked at him from head to toe, nodding with an expression that said: *yep, no mistaking it, this is the guy.*

Pastor 7 felt the pang of a cocktail of emotions boil in his gut every time he heard his name spoken:

from anguish to regret to longing. It had been months since he'd heard it. A decade earlier God had told him he was no longer who he used to be and was a new creation. Through religious study he learned that 7 is the number of completion and that each of us will get a new name when we get to heaven. Feeling reborn, David Welsh took Pastor 7 as his name on earth.

Everyone at The Garden and at his motorcycle club called him either Pastor 7 or just 7. Only people from the government used his given and surname. He could smell Federal Government all over this woman as he invited her in, then served her tea. "I thought the FBI was done with these regular check ups."

"They are. I'm Sarah Abraham. I'm with the Department of Justice—office of the Pardon Attorney."

Pardon Attorney?

"We assist the President with issuing executive clemency, and my job is to investigate each case and present it to the Pardon Attorney for his consideration. If the Pardon Attorney thinks a case has merit, he sends the Department's recommendation to the President. It is up to the President, of course, to decide whether or not to issue a pardon."

"So, what does this have to do with me? Do you need a reference or something?"

Pastor 7's complete lack of expectation tickled a broad smile from Deputy Pardon Attorney Sarah

Abraham's face: "You've been nominated for a full presidential pardon."

A pardon. The thought *had* never occurred to him. The only forgiveness that he'd been mindful of was that of the Almighty, and the ones he'd wronged throughout his life. He never imagined that the same would be on offer from the Federal Government whose duty had always been protecting its citizens—from him.

He fought back a tear that was determined to come to his eye nevertheless. "So…what do I have to do?"

"Well, I've read all the FBI records," she said while starting up her laptop and positioning her hands over its keys. "Now I want to hear your side of the story."

The ghost that was David Welsh, the one who was no more a part of him now than a movie one may have watched a decade before, was suddenly back: a demonic shadow darkening the doorway there at the pastor's residence waiting to be let back in. The last ten years had been about serving the Almighty, not himself, and he wanted to keep the door to his past shut and who he was locked away forever. But he was now being asked to open it again for the promise of redemption from the very civil society that he once subverted. "Where do you want me to start?"

"Wherever you think your story begins."

CHAPTER 2

Stalag IX-B German Prison Camp: 3 April, 1945

Flashes of welder's arc light erupted from Private Adam Welsh's eyes with each screech from the prison guard's whistle: the piercing sound waves first boring into his brain along his auditory nerve, then emerging as jagged-edged light like the high frequency frantic lines of an oscilloscope—burning with each thrust like a hot knife. The muffled clumping of his fellow POW's boots on rotting wood floors as they scrambled for roll call manifested in a flowing funnel of concentric rings—red, blue, magenta, green and back to red again—bathing his visual cortex in color. The perceived motion dizzied him, giving him vertigo and making him nauseous. He began to dry heave.

Though his comrades had put him in the center of the lower of three-high bunks to shield him from light, each time the door to the Stalag IX-B German POW barracks was swung open, the daylight slammed into his brain with the impact of a speeding freight train.

His entire head throbbed, radiating searing pain from where his shattered and indented skull pressed upon his abraded Meninges—the protective layer just mere millimeters from his swelling brain.

"We'll get your rations for you, mate," someone whispered in his ear in a cockney British accent. "Try to sleep."

Adam Welsh's war was now a private one between himself and the demons of his numerous injuries. There was hardly a part of his body that wasn't cut, bruised, bone-chipped from being thrown down on concrete or deeply scared from previous beatings. But this last demolishing at the hands of prison guards could have been his last. It had ended with a skull-crushing rifle butt to the head that laid him unconscious for days. He was fighting for his life in that bunk as much as he had on any battlefield before he was taken a prisoner of war.

Though his injuries got him moved from the tent and mud floor accommodations into the relative warmth and dryness of the barracks, his fellow prisoners thought they were only making a dying man comfortable, until he woke one day screaming. He lay for another week, fighting infection with fevers, then slowly stabilized and became conscious enough to take food.

He laid for days, sleepless in his bunk. He wanted to sleep. He welcomed sleep to come and remove him from the noise, confusion and pain emanating from his injuries. To relieve him. To gently float his consciousness down, lightly like a falling feather, to a quieter and more peaceful place. To put him out of his misery. But sleep never came. Only nightmarish daydreams did: his consciousness locked in perpetual battles, fighting for his life. Occasionally his legs would kick and arms flail with hypnic jerks as he imagined all manner of killing the guards who'd beaten him during his captivity. His fellow POWs took to restraining his clenched fists and feet, tied to his bunk with rags to prevent him from injuring himself or others. For in his mind he was gouging out their eyes with his thumbs—hearing their screams. Bayonetting them as he'd done burlap sacks filled with straw during basic training—now feeling the satisfying resistance of human flesh and bone on the blade. And hearing the camp's executioner's neck snap on the gallows at the end of a rope—seeing his head unnaturally dangling off over-stretched and torn ligaments, his body twitching as he'd seen a half-dozen allied prisoners do. He begged sleep to come.

Delirious with yet another fever, through the stench of unwashed men and un-emptied chamber-pot night buckets, he detected a distantly familiar aroma. It was burning tobacco for sure, but not the fetor of NAZI Mokri Superb Cigarettes that often wafted through the cracks between the barrack's wallboards. Though Red Cross packages contained American tobacco, it never made it to the Allied prisoners in his camp—it was stolen by the guards and either sold in a nearby town on the black market or smoked in private outside the camp. But this was American tobacco he was smelling: robust and complex, finishing with a smack akin to sweetness. It was enough to take him back to his childhood on a neighboring farm, wading through the bunches of hanging leaves in a tobacco barn where he'd hand roll cigarettes and fill his pre-teen lungs with its smoke in secret.

A clean, white armband with a red cross came into his field of view where he lay in his bunk. He'd been practically living off picked-over red cross packages from the U.S.A. for nearly a year. Were the Germans now allowing Red Cross workers to visit German POW camps too?

"We're the American 44th Infantry. You've been liberated, son," the American army medic smiled. He tried to speak, but the words would not come—only garble. The medic attempted, but then gave up trying to understand what Private Welsh was attempting to say. Rather he pulled out his dog tags, then made notes in a notepad. "Do you know what day it is, soldier? It's Tuesday," he said as he studied Private Welsh's face for some sign of recognition. "The third of April," the medic continued as he grabbed Adam Welsh's chin, gently turned his head, and with professional dispassion examined his head injury. "Nineteen hundred and forty-five." The medic administered morphine and it was finally lights out for Private Welsh: the first real sleep he'd had since the day his skull got bashed in.

When he awoke, the morphine had largely eased his psychedelic vision. He was being carried on a stretcher, and though raising his head to look around made him nauseous, he was joyful at the realization that his prison camp was being liberated by the army of Americans that now busied around him. Was the war over? Or was his POW camp only liberated by the army on its way to Berlin? Dizziness shoved him back down onto his stretcher where he could only stare upward at the dark and cloudy sky.

The prison camp's rusty, crisscrossing barbed wire archway gate, topped with a decaying wood sign rolling across his field of vision announced that he was outside the POW camp. He was free for the first time since he had dropped to his knees, raised his hands and surrendered to the enemy nearly a year earlier. And he rejoiced in the knowledge that he would survive the war, though the demons of his wartime injuries and injustices would remain. For although he was a liberated prisoner of war, his tortured soul was not saved—and his demons would never forsake him nor leave him until his dying day.

CHAPTER 3

Guaynabo Puerto Rico Federal Prison: 1999

David Welsh, begotten son of Adam Welsh, lay in his bed in solitary confinement at the Guaynabo Puerto Rico Federal Prison daydreaming of the violence to come. He was rehearsing through visualization the eye gouges, punches and kicks, elbows to the head and knees to the groin that he would use to inflict maximum damage on the gang of five prisoners who were waiting to knife him to death at first opportunity after he emerged from his cell. They would exact revenge in kind for his violent act against them—the one that had put him in solitary in the first place. But he was determined to survive this private war—whatever it took. He knew they could deal with his fighting skills, match the power of his hardened and trained body, but they would not overcome the power of his anger and hate. For David Welsh was an unsurpassed master of the weapons of anger and hate: his family legacy.

And it was the emissaries of anger and hate that David now summoned to his darkened cell like an evil wizard, a conjurer calling forth demons from the abyss of hell. He would need them soon enough: he was nearing the end of his sixty-day stretch in solitary. He reached deep for them, ever downward, all the way back to the day when, at age ten, he fought for his life against those very demons. It was the day that his father's fists of rage nearly took his life; commemorating the formal passing of the family torch of anger and hate, and their expression through violence. David had made the mistake of returning home well after suppertime to find his father in the dark, in his chair next to a nearly empty bottle of whiskey. His mother had warned him to steer clear of his father when he drank alone. "It's that damned war," she would tell him. And David did his best to discreetly bypass him on his way to the kitchen. But through the shadows he could see his father's eyes turn to track him like the eyes of a hungry predator from inside a cave. They were as dark and empty as two bottomless holes, gateways to eternity, a window into the chamber of hell where souls were tortured. Terrified to the core David could only freeze and stand and shiver with fear as the demons of anger and hate brought his father to his feet and across the room to him.

The next thing David could recall was running from the house, too terrified to look back and disappearing into a nearby forest. Alone, battered and bloody he washed the blood from his skin and his clothes there in a creek as best he could. Exhausted and frightened and in terrible physical and emotional pain this boy found what he could to make himself comfortable enough to sleep. Over the next few days he followed the creek for miles until he found a flat area with enough debris to make a lean-to and basic shelter. And it was there that he would live for another two years.

And his anger and his hate grew.

He would spend his days hiding from truancy officers, and when the coast was clear, steal clothes off clothes lines, break into homes for food and into cars to steal items to sell for cash. And when school was finished he would hop the fence into a nearby apartment complex where he'd laugh and play with the children there, none of them ever suspecting that when the call came for them to come home for supper, little David would hop back over the fence and snug himself into the collection of scrap materials that he called home down by the creek. Some days he would earn an invitation from one of the neighborhood boys to come to their house for supper. He always minded his manners in the presence of these families, but only barely kept the anger within him in check. But he didn't hate them for what they had, he only hated that he didn't have what they did: a caring mother and father, a home life where people treated each other with decency. He left their home smiling and with a thank you. But when he thought of where he used to call home, where there resided a battle-scarred ogre with anger and hate in his heart and a metal plate in his head, his own anger and hate and despair would return to cower with him there in his hovel by the creek.

And his anger and hate grew even more.

And there was more indignation to be gleaned from his early teen years that would help him fight for his survival once he was released from solitary into the general population. He thought of his first incarceration at age 13 when he was finally picked up by truancy officers and put into a juvenile facility. Illiterate and nearly socially feral, he lashed out with the only tool he knew: violence. And with each subsequent act of violence he perpetrated, he was driven deeper and one step closer to total self-destruction.

And his anger and hate grew still more.

His penchant for violence led to his first incarceration in adult prison at age 15. He was already a hair trigger just waiting for a reason to set off an inner charge of explosive anger and hate. To victimize the victimizers who subjected him to the imbrues, abuses and injustices of his incarceration. And even more anger and hate poured into his tightly clenched fists there on that bed, in that solitary cell in Guaynabo.

But there was room in David's heart for more anger and hate, still.

Not just any ordinary anger, though. Not his life-long anger at the abuses of his father, nor that born of his emotional pain would do. And neither the prejudices of his jailers, nor the injustices of their system. No. This would require a special anger and he used the recollection of his latest sentencing to awaken it: "…this court sentences you to 25 years to life in prison…" It was his anger at himself. At what he had done to his life, for in his heart he knew that this last sentence was just.

He was fully charged now with anger and hate that welled up from within like a tidal wave when he heard footsteps in the solitary corridor. The sound of dangling keys made his already racing heart race faster. This was it. It was time. A gladiator prepared to enter the Roman Colosseum. *We who are about to die salute you*. He was ready.

But the keys went into the door next to his cell's. And it was another prisoner whom the guards spoke with in muffled voices outside his steel cell door before fading down the corridor. It was not his time.

What would he do now so flush with anger and hate? There would be no releasing them alone there in his cell. So ready to perform his artful and specular acts of violence, and to inflict great bodily harm on that gang of five. He needed to somehow send the demons he'd summoned back to hell, for now.

But instead of winding down, his heart began to race even faster. Though his cell was dark, an eerie light suddenly filled his vision and he could see in the dark every detail of his cell—every corner no matter how deeply shadowed, every stone on the floor no matter how small, every scratch in the wall no matter how shallow, and every smudge on his cell door no matter how faint—he could see as if his eyes were projecting a light upon them. His perception of his surroundings became surreal while his pent-up energy suddenly fell off as if a high-revving engine had blown and ground to a stop. The physical world around him began to fade as if it were a mere dream, becoming as phony as the set of a stage play—and he was returned to another reality that hadn't been revealed to him since before the day he was born. He was facing eternity again. Weakness overtook his muscles and he was unable to move. He sat on his bed, motionless, helpless as a terrible fear overcame and enveloped him.

He was not alone in that cell.

The walls of his increasingly flimsy and translucent cell had degraded to become barely more substantial than the flickering images of an old-time motion picture show, when five dark and bottomless shadows manifested into recognizable humanoid shapes before him. The world of sound and words became as irrelevant as if he were floating in outer space. His consciousness received understanding loud and clear: while these demons were on their way back to hell as he now willed them, they weren't leaving without him.

Fear transformed into terror as he felt them pulling his soul from his body over the horizon of a black hole and into the abyss. Their spiritual touch lasted for a mere fragment of eternity, but during which he experienced his father's entire lifetime of torment at the hands of these demons. There was a familiarity. They knew him. And they knew he knew they knew him. And that they had come to collect his soul and take him to hell.

David instantly regressed into a child-like state and regained just enough strength to throw himself down on his knees and to reach his arms into the air. And amidst perfect silence, with echoless recording-studio clarity, he heard his own voice: "I surrender."

At that instant he felt a hand on his right shoulder and the words spoken directly into his heart: "I will never leave you nor forsake you."

CHAPTER 4

David again heard ringing keys, but this time against his cell's door: it was his turn to return to the prison's general population. And to the arms of the gang of five.

But now he was unarmed. Gone from his cell were the demons. Gone from his heart were his weapons of anger and hate forged so long ago in the fire of his pain, tempered to hardness by his loneliness and sharpened with the despair that he'd lived with from the day he escaped his father. It was all gone. It was replaced with something new that not only filled his heart, but gushed through to overflowing. A wellspring that emanated from his being now surged through him, erupting from deep within him like a great fountain. Something new and strange to him, but very welcome. The pure love of The Holy Spirit.

The cell door swung open revealing two guards wearing stab vests who stood holding billy clubs and Tasers at the ready. But they stared at David sitting there placidly on his bed and seemed immediately disarmed with apprehension. This wasn't the man they'd put in this cell sixty days earlier. He was a raging animal: furious with blood in his eyes and someone else's blood on his shirt and hands. But now they sensed something different in this prisoner. Peace.

David stood and calmly walked to the door, turned and offered his hands behind his back to the guards for handcuffing—David knew the procedure. And so did the guards, but in their befuddlement from this man's radiating utter tranquility one of the guards absentmindedly scrambled for his handcuffs and gently placed them around David's wrists.

"He's all yours," said one of the solitary confinement guards who had escorted him to the prison canteen. "Go easy," he asked of the general population guard as he handed him a clipboard for signing David Welsh's transfer of custody out of solitary. "He's been in for 60."

"Welsh," recited the receiving guard, not making eye contact with David. "Chow time. You got 30 minutes before we take you to your new cell."

Released from his handcuffs and slowly walking into the canteen David could hear one of the guards comment under his breath to the other: "Is your guy still taking five-to-one odds?"

His fellow prisoners and other guards busied themselves not looking at David. Not when he got his food in the cafeteria. And not when he sat down at an empty table in the dining area. Men, who still had food on their plates at the tables next to him, picked up and left. The normal din of prisoners eating was muted to scattered conversations in low tones. David put his head down and began to eat.

Upon reaching for his dessert David heard the room fall silent and motionless: just as he had observed the way birds, and squirrels, rabbits and other small forest mammals froze in their tracks and clung closely to tree trunks or other nearby objects whenever a pair of nesting eagles would return to their nest above the lean-to shelter that he'd lived in for nearly two years. A top predator had arrived on the scene.

David didn't need to look up to see that not a single guard was in the room, and that the gang of five, leader and his cohorts, were seated atop a table across the room. David could feel them watching him, but kept eating. Finishing what he reckoned could be his last supper, David wiped his mouth, stood and walked directly to the gang: making, then not breaking eye contact with its leader.

As he approached, the gang leader pursed his lips, shifted slightly on his perch atop their table, and nodded while issuing a look of cold-blooded murder from his eyes. He squinted at David. "You."

"Me," David nodded, fearless and at peace—completely disarmed in his heart.

While the two men stared at each other in silence, David could see out of the corners of his eyes the other four gangsters looking back and forth between him and their leader. Searching, David supposed, for a cue as to what to do next.

The words came from his mouth voluntarily, but seemingly not under his direction: "The Holy Spirit is within me."

The gangster squinted more deeply at him as he presented an exaggerated nod while drawing and releasing a long breath.

"If you and your amigos do me harm, you don't have to worry about what I'm going to do to you. What you have to worry about is the wrath of God that will come to you afterward." David not only spoke in a non-threatening way, he was imploring them as if he were talking a jumper down from a window's ledge.

The gang leader only stared at David. Though his war face was fixed, his eyes betrayed fear—something that David had learned to recognize in his earlier trade.

"I will never be left nor forsaken by Him," David said pouring kindness through his eyes, and opening his arms to make himself vulnerable to whatever the gangsters had planned for him. "I am ready to meet my maker now if that is what He wills." The gang-leader's perplexed expression at what was now happening before him confirmed that more than just the general idea had gotten through their language barrier. "If I live past this moment, then I will live for

Him. If I die now, I will join Him in heaven," smiling, palms up and arms open.

"You God man now?" The gang leader said while stiffening his demeanor against whatever was going on in his heart and mind, but he still couldn't conceal his fear from David.

"God man now."

The gang leader leapt to his feet. "God man," he hissed in false mockery from behind his brave façade, flashing gangster signs as he strutted away—his bewildered gang in tow.

David would never know for certain whether it was superstition or reverence for The Holy Spirit that caused the gang leader to walk away. Only that what happened that day was the will of The Holy Spirit that now dwelled within him.

"You wait here," the guard escorting David said while pulling him from the line of prisoners returning to their cells and standing him at the cellblock entrance door. David stood for nearly 30 minutes before a pair of guards walked past him, one carrying a shrink-wrapped hygiene kit and the other opening one of the cell doors further down the block. There was a commotion inside that he couldn't see from his angle, but he could hear cussing. Moments later, a protesting prisoner was escorted out of the cell in the other direction, carrying his possessions in a cardboard box.

"Welsh!" Shouted the guard standing just outside the cell, who was gesturing for him to now walk to the open cell door. The bed was stripped and atop the bare mattress laid the hygiene kit. "You'll get sheets and more clothing issued tomorrow."

David sat on his bed. His cellmate was lying with his back turned, reading a book and paid him no mind. He rolled back onto the mattress and stared at the paint chips clinging to the ceiling; casting and retrieving long jagged shadows at the behest of a tired and flickering florescent light. And although he had every reason at that moment to despair over now truly ranking among the last, the lost and the least, rather, his heart was overflowing with joy and he was at peace.

* * *

"They never planned on you needing a bed. Or a cell," said deputy Pardon Attorney Sarah Abraham as she looked up from her laptop wearing a look of astonishment in the office of the pastor's residence of The Garden. "They were trying to get you killed,"

David nodded, wearing a peaceful smile.

"Why?"

"After 25 years in and out of the system, I was deemed a lost cause. An incorrigible," David said without breaking his smile. "The system had only one use for me: informant."

"Inform on your former associates?"

"Them. And the people I was in prison with. Anybody that could be useful to them. But I wouldn't do it, you see."

"So, your transfer to Guaynabo was supposed to be your death sentence."

"Yes, either to scare me into rolling over or to be eliminated. Either way. But they didn't count on God."

CHAPTER 5

David busied himself rotating his hands in the way he'd learned over the years to keep the blood flowing through his wrists under tight handcuffs. Through the expanded metal cage and windshield of the transfer van David saw a sign on the guard house they had stopped at: United States Penitentiary, Atlanta.

"You won't be here long, Welsh," said the guard driving the van, while glancing at the guard in the passenger seat next to him. "Yeah. Atlanta is used as a transfer prison," the other guard said optimistically, looking back at the driver and nodding. David could decode from their expressions and silent glances as they stepped from the transfer van that they weren't telling him the entire story.

David closed his eyes and listened intently. He could barely hear the guards' conversation outside with the gatehouse attendant, but some of their conversation managed to get through: "…see how the black Muslims like him…." And "…last stop."

His last stop. There had been many last stops for David, but none like his first adult prison. Anguished and alone in the world, the first night was the worst: struggling to fall asleep atop a fetid bare mattress breathing against ribs fractured from the beating he'd taken from his *cellie*, while replaying images of the sinister, predatory looks that the other inmates in the cellblock had given him through the bars when he'd entered the cellblock earlier. Looking at the five-year stretch that lay ahead of him that day, he was convinced that he'd never survive five days—let alone five years.

But he did, at a price. A sanctioned knifing that cost him a stretch in solitary got him into the good graces of one of the most notorious biker-gang drug and crime syndicates in the southeastern United States: American Mongrels. While other crime organizations, biker gangs in particular, segregated themselves by race, the Mongrels were true to their name and accepted anyone who had the potential to be an earner. They didn't have time for the race-war nonsense: there was no money in it. Half Cherokee and half Welsh, David fit the bill. Upon completing his first sentence in adult prison he would ride away from his first *last stop* on a chopper—the first thing he'd ever owned—courtesy of the Mongrels.

A year on the outside and he'd received the obligatory Mongrel basic membership tattoos, wore the requisite colors and facial hair, and he'd completed further initiation rites that included participating in a bank robbery and a battle in a turf war. David was only 22 by that time but, consistently hitting his monthly financial goals from his assigned protection racket territory, he was quickly on his way up in his life of crime. With each wrung of the ladder he earned the right to bear a particular tattoo—accumulating and displaying them like soldiers' commendation and campaign ribbons—until only a fully buttoned long sleeve shirt and long pants would cover them all.

"Mmmm, ummm. They are just going to love them tats in here in USP Atlanta," the receiving prison guard conducting the strip search said as he shook his head while examining David. "Ain't no white supremacist going to make friends in here. Uh-huh. No way, no how." David just hoped that the inmates were better at deciphering his tattoos and distinguishing them from those of a white supremacist's.

* * *

"Don't eat the soup, I heard someone pissed in it earlier," announced the gaunt, nasally inmate everyone called Weasel, as he joined the table of five where David sat. "It was probably one of them black Muslims. They don't eat anything unless it's kosher."

"Halal," grumbled Whitey, the hulking old inmate who seemed to have lost all pigment in his hair and skin due to age, lack of exposure to the sun owing to long-term incarceration, or both.

"Yeah, whatever. What I'm saying is they've got their own food, so it must have been one of them who did it."

“Don’t start nothin’ with the blacks,” said Whitey through a mouthful of bread. Swallowing: “I’m telling you, I won’t be there to back you up if you start something with them black Muslims.”

“Besides,” spoke up another diner, “…it could just as easily been one of the guards who did it.”

David used his napkin to cover the bowl of soup on the far corner of his tray. But he wasn’t concerned about food. Rather, he had another, insatiable hunger to deal with: hunger for the knowledge of the one who had reached him in that solitary cell in Guaynabo and pulled him back from the edge of hell. The peace in his heart had never left him nor forsaken him since that moment on that day, but whoever it was who had renewed his life—rebirthed him—remained a mystery. And he had been on a mission to find Him ever since.

David felt an urgent kick to his shin under the table and he looked up from his musings to see a half dozen black gangbangers patrolling the dining area moving serpentine as they strutted their way through the dining hall between the tables. The scene resembled that of a scuba excursion in Mexico during one of his better days with the Mongrels. They’d had a good year and the higher-ranking members decided they’d ride the length of Baja Mexico together. David had just been promoted to a junior officer and was eligible to go. While diving on a reef there he felt a hand gently pull him down to the sandy bottom. He looked around to see that it was the dive instructor who had done so, and he and the rest of the dive class were congregated on the sand behind a large coral head. When the dive instructor pointed off to the distance David turned and saw a pack of a half-dozen or so large barracuda slinking through the coral outcroppings. Over six feet in length, they were a fearsome-looking fish and they passed by close enough for David to see their cold doll's eyes roaming the landscape, mouths agape, their distinctive grotesque underbite revealing needle-like teeth. Predators just like the ones who were slinking past him in the prison's dining hall, before disappearing through the door that led to the basketball courts.

Watching it all was a group of men spread among three tables, all wearing *kufi* caps atop their heads. The black Muslims. As one who had been blind his entire life and who was now suddenly made to see by The Holy Spirit, David now noticed things about them that he hadn't when encountering black Muslims in other prisons he'd occupied over the years. Their body language and style showed nothing of *the street* from where they came. David noted the congenial way they behaved toward one other and the disciplined way they ate—like the families he would eat with when he was a runaway. The clarity and cleanliness in the way they spoke the English language. He also noticed that not all the black Muslims were black: there was a middle eastern-looking man and a white man among them.

Someone at the table must have noticed David studying the black Muslims. "Mustafa, the biggest one. The older one in the middle. He's the boss," David was informed through an anonymous whisper. David made eye contact with Mustafa. Both men regarded each other with brief, expressionless gazes then looked elsewhere.

* * *

The sixty-day stretch in Guaynabo solitary had weakened David physically. An afternoon spent weightlifting in USP Atlanta's weight room found him struggling to bench press over two-hundred seventy pounds, where he'd regularly bench pressed over three-hundred fifty pounds before. His muscle and body build were an important part of his earlier trade, be it for intimidation effect when collecting during a shakedown, or in actual physical application when breaking bones and popping joints. It was also insurance against anyone in prison getting the idea that he was up for grabs. But none of that mattered to him anymore. He feared nothing. He wanted for nothing. All that mattered to him was The Holy Spirit that had now completely displaced the violent, feral creature that once inhabited his body, soul and persona—and his mission to find his Redeemer.

It was time for cardio and sport, and David moved with the crowd to the basketball courts. The prison court consisted of two full courts laid out in a crossways fashion which, except during formal competitions, were most often used as four half-courts. Invariably a ball would get away from one set of players, roll into another's area and interrupt play. Most days this was not contested.

"What the hell?" said one of the barracuda who was hit in the calf with a ball from David's court. "I know you white boys can't jump, but you'd better keep the ball on your own court if you know what's right for you." He kicked the ball off the court.

"Go 'n get it," ordered Weasel, who was instantly surrounded by six barracuda who were ready to bite. Weasel stupidly stood his ground.

"Oh, damn," Whitey moaned. "I told that moron not to...."

David quickly walked over to the impending brawl, reached into the center of the huddle, grabbed Weasel by the collar and pulled him out of danger. "Forget about this fool," he said to the angry faces that turned on him ready to pounce. He disarmed them with: "He doesn't have the sense God gave a dog."

David dipped the mop into the bucket, then squeezed out dirty water in the wringer. He had half a corridor left and decided that he needed to refresh the water back at the sink in the janitor's closet. He turned to see three figures approaching from down the corridor with determination in their stride. He didn't need to look the other direction to know that at least as many barracuda were closing in from behind.

"You think you own the place, you white supremacist mother?" The meanest looking barracuda said, his face close enough for David to smell his bad breath.

David stood still. Tranquil and relaxed.

"Do you see any of your KKK inbred kin around here? Ain't none of you lasted more than a week in USP, Atlanta. We seen to that."

"These are American Mongrel tattoos," David spoke calmly, neither defensive nor pleading. He instantly recognized the anger and hate emanating from these men: the very demons that The Holy Spirit had wrenched him from at the edge of hell. He could feel their presence, wanting to pull him back in, to supplant the tranquility in his heart with their evil essence. But there was no way he would ever let them back in. And he knew the demons knew it and wanted to destroy him for it.

Another barracuda took the mop from his hand and broke the handle under his knee, instantly creating a jagged stab weapon. For the old David, that would have been *his* first move when he saw them approaching. But he didn't do it. Nor did he clench his fists or raise his arms in defense. He knew in his heart that The Holy Spirit would either protect him, or bring him to a better place. He welcomed either outcome. He truly feared no evil.

"Back up," the bellowing voice of Mustafa ordered, so deep and rich in tone that David could practically feel it in his breastbone as it reverberated down the concrete corridor.

Mustafa approached the scene dressed in his sheer, flowing white *thobe* and kufi having just come from sunset prayer. He was a physically imposing man, but his authoritative charisma was his primary armament.

"This man is not a white supremacist," he preached to the barracuda. Mustafa looked deeply into David's eyes, probing him. "I don't know what he is, but he isn't that."

"He needs to learn respect," one of the barracuda barked.

Mustafa glowered at the man who'd spoken. "Respect? You don't know the meaning of the word, son. Respect begins with humility before Allah and following the teachings of the prophet Muhammad."

"Sheeeesh, not that again," dismissed the lead barracuda, whose mob turned together with him like a school of fish before slowly swimming away down the corridor—their egos bruised, but intact.

"Thank you. I only wish to be left in peace."

Five of Mustafa's flock arrived in near panic, but slowed to a walk when they realized that there was no threat to their teacher. Nevertheless, David drew angry stares from them. Mustafa put them at ease: "It is alright, my brothers."

Looking at David: "What is it about you…"

"David."

"David." Mustafa repeated. "What are *you* doing in here?"

"I've hurt a lot of people in my life. That is why I've been put in here: to protect other people from me. But now I've been filled with The Holy Spirit and am looking for the one who saved me from hell."

Mustafa's followers appeared shocked. "The Ruh al-Qudus," one of them whispered to Mustafa.

"You are seeking The Holy Spirit?

"I was visited by The Holy Spirit and He hasn't left me or forsaken me ever since."

"Jibrayil?" one of them looked at another.

Mustafa bore a doubtful but inquisitive expression. "In Arabic al-Qudus translates The Holy One. Jibrayil, his created messenger."

David listened intently.

"Have you read the Qur'an. The religious text of Islam?"

"I never learned to read." David had said those words many times throughout his life—to parole officers and counselors alike. That admission was always the source of his worst shame. But now they were benign to him. Painless.

"It is the word of Allah." Mustafa must have realized that David would almost certainly not recognize the name. He translated: "It is the word of God."

David's heart sang at the revelation that The Holy Spirit, God, had left his word for humanity to read. He had been aching for word from his Savior and here it was in something as simple as a book. "I want to know this book."

Mustafa regarded David for a moment, appearing to be weighing his authenticity. "Islam is about being reborn. It turned us all from hardened criminals into men of God you see before you now."

"Yes. Reborn. That is what happened to me. But I know nothing about God. Will you teach me?"

"Our Islamic faith, our culture, is based on community, discipline and ritual prayer. Becoming a Muslim is a reversion. It takes us back to our natural state under the laws of Allah. When you become a Muslim you come home among your brothers," Mustafa opened his arms to include his flock that surrounded him.

When David escaped to live two years feral he not only lost any semblance of a normal life, he lost his family in the process. As bad as his family was, it was still home. And no matter how old he got, no matter how tall he grew, no matter how much muscle he put on, and no matter how many scars he earned, he was always and still that lost ten-year-old boy looking for his way home. A home he couldn't ever return to.

"Please take me home," David uttered meekly as he stood there, trembling, sniffing back tears.

"Welcome home, brother," Mustafa said as he embraced the 6 foot 3 inch, two-hundred-fifty pound scared and lost ten-year-old boy.

"Allahu Akbar," some of Mustafa's flock whispered.

* * *

"Welsh, prayer time," the guard said through the bars before unlocking his cell door. "You're on the list. You are going to this thing, right?" the guard said apprehensively. David figured he didn't fit the guard's profile of the Muslim prisoners he'd overseen: long, slightly greying blond hair in a ponytail reaching down to the center of his back, blue eyes, biker gang tattoos—his persona was all wrong. David nodded, rose to his feet and quietly marched together with the faithful.

Mustafa was waiting at the prayer room entrance door greeting everyone who entered with a smile and comment in Arabic that David didn't understand. He smiled broadly when he saw David and took his hand with both hands. "Brother David. Today is your special day. Be sure to sit up front."

David made his way to the front row amid smiles and well wishes of "welcome brother."

Once the room filled and doors closed Mustafa turned to David. "Brother David, if you would please rise and stand against the wall to my left," he gestured. David obliged and what unfolded before him was in his eyes strange and mystical. He watched in fascination as the men kneeling on their prayer rugs first stood, then bowed, then prostrated themselves, finishing sitting on their feet on the ground. During each of these postures they recited what David could only surmise were verses from their Qur'an and prayers. Mustafa spoke from a podium about things David couldn't yet understand, before taking a few minutes to share news and information with the group. Mustafa then let the room fall into silence while he adjusted his clothes and composed himself with a short, silent prayer.

"Today we welcome our brother into the nation of Islam," all eyes turned to David as Mustafa raised his hand and gestured for him to stand beside him. "I saw something good in you. Your peace and tranquility mostly. But something else. A longing. An insatiable desire. A spiritual longing. The al-Qudus, The Holy One, touched you and sent you to us. You wish to no longer be what you were. You wish to have everything you've done before wiped away. You wish to be a new person. Allah willing, you will be born again in Islam."

"I do," David pleaded with all his heart.

"To be Muslim you must believe in God and that there is no God except Allah, the creator of everything. And the prophet Muhammad—peace be on him—is his messenger."

"I will."

"To be Muslim you must observe the Athaan, the call to prayer five times a day: at dawn, mid-day, late afternoon, sunset, and at night, just before lights out. The Salat, Muslim prayer, and learn how to pray to Allah."

"I will."

"To be Muslim you must practice Zakah. Charity as a form of purification. You must give 2.5% of your savings, once a year to the poor."

"I will."

"To be Muslim you must Saum. Fast. Fasting brings us closer to Allah. During the month of Ramadhan, you will eat only once in the morning, and then again when the sun goes down. Saum is a self-discipline that helps us control ourselves and keep away the sins of greed and selfishness. It reminds us never to forget the poor and those in need.

"I will."

"To be Muslim, if you can afford it and have the physical ability, you must perform the Hajj at least once in your lifetime during the Islamic month of Dhu al-Hijjah. You will make this holy pilgrimage—the Hajj—to Makkah, in Saudi Arabia: the heart of our Islamic world and the birthplace of both the Prophet Muhammad and our Muslim religion.

"I will." The thought occurred to David that lifers among them would never be able to make the trip—and wondered if a life sentence in prison would qualify as an exemption. But he quickly put that thought out of his mind.

"Allahu Akbar," the flock chanted in unison, surprising David. He has just been taught and promised to fulfill the five pillars of Islam.

Mustafa took David by both hands and faced him squarely. "It is time to recite your passage and enter the nation of Islam, brother. And you will be born again."

"Allahu Akbar," was spoken in hushed tones scattered throughout the room.

Mustafa had prepared David earlier for the ritual by having him memorize the declaration in Arabic:

"I bear witness that there is no God but Allah and Mohammed is his messenger."

"Allahu Akbar!" David was bathed in smiles and hugs from everyone in the room. He was presented with a thobe, which he pulled over his head, before donning and adjusted his new kufi on his head. He was given a Qur'an and kissed on both cheeks.

"David," Mustafa said smiling. "Your name is Abrahamic, but nevertheless we'll see about selecting an appropriate Muslim name for you."

* * *

David still felt uneasy about his inability to read the Qur'an: either in Arabic or English. He tried, but the writing simply wouldn't become words and words wouldn't become sentences. So, like he'd done all his life, he would listen intently to others, memorize and recite what he'd heard—all to conceal his inability to read. He didn't need to hide that now, amongst his Muslim brothers. They accepted him as he was. And many of them were learning to read too. But his illiteracy nevertheless brought him a tinge of shame now because he couldn't even read the word of the one who'd saved him. Under the tutelage of Mustafa and some of his Muslim brothers, David had managed to memorize many prayers for just about any occasion. Although sermons and teachings from the Qur'an were spoken in English, and Mustafa was a gifted teacher, still so many words were unfamiliar to him that he always felt behind the curve. But David was committed to learning the word of God—The Holy Spirit who had saved him. After all, Islam taught that sloth is a sin.

David had spent the earlier part of the morning practicing reciting prayers that he had been memorizing from a cassette tape available through the prison library. He would be ready to please Mustafa with new recitations at the day's Mid-Day Prayer.

"Allahu Akbar!" David heard men shouting down the cellblock from his cell.

Other voices rose too, but they were secular voices: tirades filled with profanity and anger. Something big was going on in the cellblock.

Guards ran past David's open cell door as a blaring TV joined the cacophony rolling through the cellblock. David rose from his bunk and flowed with the crowd down the stairs to the common area where prisoner and guard alike were gathered in front of a TV set that was encased within an expanded metal cage.

"They flew damned planes into the World Trade Center…both towers," one of the guards shouted.

"Our brothers have risen up to destroy our enemies: the Great Satan of Christendom."

"Shut the hell up," one of the secular prisoners with an Army Airborne tattoo on his forearm shouted back.

"They've been after those buildings since the 1993 bombing," another guard said, shaking his head.

"Brothers: the battle for the caliphate has begun," one of the younger and more aggressive of David's Muslim brothers said.

Caliphate? David, knew the word, but only in the historical context in which Mustafa had taught him: an Islamic kingdom under a Muslim ruler.

"I told you to shut the hell up," the Army Airborne tattoo barked back.

Ranks quickly closed and faced off: Muslims versus secular.

"We have been called to arms, brothers…"

"Stop!" Mustafa interrupted with his powerful voice. "Shut your mouth…now," he ordered.

Tension in the room was palpable as a massive brawl was about to break out. "Please, take us to the prayer room, now," Mustafa said to the guards with a calm urgency.

"Yeah, Okay. Good idea," the guard responded. "All of you, to the prayer room. The rest of you back to your cells. Now."

As the two groups went their separate directions, David was torn. Which way should *he* go? Mustafa settled it for him by gently putting his arm around David's shoulder and leading him away together with his Muslim brothers. David looked back long enough to see the dirty looks and disgust at him on the faces of the secular prisoners.

When they arrived, the prayer room was boiling with excited voices and laughter. "Death to America," several men began chanting in Arabic.

"Come on, David," seeing that he was not celebrating, one of the young hot heads grabbed David by the shoulders. "This is *our* victory against the man. The ones who kept you down. The ones who took everything you had. The ones that tried to destroy your life before you came to Islam."

But by the grace of The Holy Spirit David had learned in his heart that no man had made his life what it once was. And at that moment The Holy Spirit made his eyes to see the unseen, revealing to him through the angry faces and expressions of hostility of the men, just who had destroyed his earlier life: the demons of anger and hate. They were back. He could smell them, like the stench of death, they were revealed through the fetid furor that filled the room. He could feel them longing for his soul, reaching out, beckoning to him, enticing him to let them back into his heart. But David refused them, again.

Mustafa responded to the scene with anger. "You think this is a victory?" he bellowed. The room fell silent as he walked up to the podium in silence as his flock settled on the floor with bemused faces. "This will bring about the deaths of far more Muslims than it will infidels."

Though David had heard Mustafa use the term infidel in the abstract when referring to non-Muslims during his teachings, it was the first time he'd heard him use the term infidel to describe a specific people. In this case, Americans.

"Just what do you think they are going to do about it, huh?"

The term *they* stuck uncomfortably in David's gut: was he a they? Or one of them?

"Death to the infidel!" Shouted one of his flock, echoed by calls of "Allahu Akbar!"

"Shut your mouths and think one step ahead. What will they now do in defense? How many Muslims will die now? Surely they will attack our Muslim homelands in response."

"None of us wants Muslims to die, Mustafa. But if killing the infidel gets us what we want…"

"You fool," Mustafa shot back. "This has only put them on the defensive now. This is a setback in the cause of a world caliphate. This is not the way. The world caliphate must come peacefully. The infidel must be walked into the nation of Islam. Not blown up into it."

World caliphate? Did they really intend to bring about a worldwide Islamic state?

* * *

"Sunset. Prayer time, Welsh." The guard said between the bars.

David just shook his head in the negative and the guard moved on.

David removed his kufi from his now shaven head and placed it atop his neatly folded thobe after changing back into regular prison garb. He then laid his Qur'an atop it all and stared at them, piled up at the end of his bed.

A while later he caught the attention of the prison counselor as he was walking past his cell. He picked up his clothes and Qur'an and passed them through the bars.

"Would you take these to the prayer room, please. I won't be needing them anymore."

CHAPTER 6

David stared out the window as their Justice Prisoner and Alien Transportation System (JPATS) Boeing 727 glided toward the plains of Oklahoma. He saw combines harvesting farmland, trucks plying interstates and a dozen hot air balloons at various stages of lift-off out toward the horizon. David was pleased that there still was a world beyond cellblocks and lights out, prison food and screams in the middle of the night, and ankle cuff chains that tethered him to the airplane floor and handcuffs that bound one hand to his armrest.

"Uh, ladies and gentlemen, we are on our final approach to the Federal Transfer Center at Oklahoma City's Will Rogers World Airport. Please raise your seat backs and tray tables to their upright and locked positions and turn off any electronic devices." The guard at the forward section of the cabin smirked at the snide announcements. "We know you didn't have a choice of airlines today and, whether you are staying in Oklahoma or wherever your final destination is today or in the afterlife, we want to thank you for choosing Con Air and hope you never fly with us again in the future." The pilot did not manage to key off his microphone before it picked up laughter in the cockpit. None of David's fellow prisoners shared their sense of humor.

David saw a large Native American sand painting Thunderbird on the side of a mound out near the airport fence that quickly passed by as they touched down and began to roll to a stop. Oklahoma is Indian country.

"Welsh, you're half Injun, right?" said one of the guards who came back into the main cabin to begin preparing the prisoners for deplaning.

"Uh-huh."

"Well, then…welcome home."

* * *

David didn't think that the Federal Correctional Institution El Rino felt any more like home than any other federal prison. But he did long for home: his spiritual home. The grace of The Holy Spirit who now guided him told his heart that it not only existed but was waiting for him to discover. Puerto Rico, Atlanta, Oklahoma, or behind bars, on the street, six feet under, wherever his body was made no difference to him now. Only where his soul was and where it was going—his mission to know The Holy Spirit.

FCL El Rino was a respite for David from having to endure yet another new-prisoner gauntlet of negotiating turf domains and settling in among tangled alliances. Everyone seemed to pretty much keep to themselves at El Rino, owing to it being a relatively *clean* facility: that is, absence of a significant gang presence and prisoner hierarchy.

There was a hierocracy, though: of an eclectic mix of Native American shaman, priests and holy men, as a result of Oklahoma having been the final stop for many native American tribes that had been relocated from around the country.

And at the top of that hierocracy was Old Joe, a man who fit every stereotypical image of the modern-day native American: slicked-back hair, glints buried between deep eye wrinkles peering through amber aviator prescription glasses, gaunt sunken cheeks, all atop a lanky frame actuated by taut, cable-like muscles stretched under mottled paper-thin greasy brown skin. He spoke through a heavy Native American accent, and though they'd stood side-by-side in the cafeteria line and walked past each other in the yard a dozen times, he completely ignored David. That is, until the day he walked up to David in the prison yard.

"You are on a spiritual journey."

Taking him completely by surprise, David only managed to look at Old Joe.

"I can see that you are searching."

David had heard other inmates talk about Old Joe. They said he had one foot in the spiritual world and one in the material world at all times. That he was an exceptional medium in this regard and was often visited by visions. David never listened to superstition. If it didn't help him survive in this world he'd never had time for it. He reflexively fell into his defensive mode and planned to not give Old Joe the time of day.

"The Great Spirit has spoken to you and now you are trying to find him."

David was listening.

Old Joe grinned at whatever expression now shown on David's face.

"Yes. I've been filled with The Holy Spirit and am looking for the one who saved me from hell."

"But you don't know him. And you don't know where to find him."

David nodded.

"That is because you are looking for him in the white man's world. You won't find him there. But he brought you here so you can find him and be closer to him. To be at his side."

David's guard dropped completely. He couldn't restrain his longing to be with the one who'd saved him from those demons in that Guaynabo solitary cell.

"His name is Wakan Tanka, The Great Spirit."

"Waken Tanka," David repeated in a whisper. Was he actually speaking his name? The one?

"But you are trapped in the white man's world. You need a spiritual guide to take you to him, to where *he* resides. In *our* world," Old Joe smiled broadly through ruddy, jumbled teeth. "Do you want to meet him?"

David felt his heart move to his throat. He wanted nothing else.

* * *

Old Joe had a duty to prepare David to meet The Great Spirit. He explained to David that he was unclean and needed to complete a series of purification rituals before performing the final ceremony that would have him meet his maker. Old Joe was an equal opportunity spiritualist and had David partake in purification ceremonies that were as diverse as the Native American tribes that had brought them to Oklahoma. The sweat lodge, was one. The medicine lodge, another. A Navajo medicine man who routinely visited the prison to serve the spiritual needs of several Navajo inmates led them in a sand painting ceremony. And Smudging, or smoke purification, among still several others. From his native Cherokee traditions he learned more about The Great Spirit.

"He is the one who lives above," Old Joe raised his palms to the sky. "He is the all-powerful and all-knowing creator of all things. He oversees everything across the universe: including people."

David delighted that The Great Spirit created the heavens and the earth. Mother earth: to feed her children—people—and look after their needs. To provide light so that we may see and darkness that we may sleep. Water for us to drink and dry land for us to walk upon. Plants and animals to eat and the very air we breathe. All so that we may live.

And then there was the Ghost Dance. Another gift from The Great Spirit.

"The Caddo Nation practices it best," Old Joe explained as he nodded to the proud Caddo shaman seated with them in the makeshift medicine lodge in the prison yard. "It is a tool he gave us not too long ago, when we were losing our connection to mother earth because of the white man's deeds to separate us from her."

Indian—white man. Was that the source of internal conflict that troubled David all his life? That troubled his family? Two disparate stands of cultural DNA forced together that could never achieve cultural meiosis and stable offspring? The violent conflicts within his own family of the same source that manifested violence between Indian and white man?

"The dance is a bridge to the spiritual world," Old Joe explained. To commune with those who've departed the physical world, but remain in their eternal spirits. "They are not lost to us. We just didn't know how to communicate with them. It is the Ghost Dance that gives us a way. And the spirits tell us that the world as we know it today will soon end and be restored. Reborn a pure world without white men." David's heart filled with joy at the prospect of his native peoples returning to live in peace and harmony with mother earth, for her to nurture them the way she once did. When the dead resurrect and together they'd live eternally, without suffering. When they would all be in heaven on earth.

"But I am half white man."

"Do not be disheartened, my son," Old Joe put his calloused and weathered hand atop David's. "All believers will be resurrected. You only need to believe," Old Joe smiled.

David felt the weight of despair lift from his shoulders. The Great Spirit was giving him a way to salvation. He now saw the power and wisdom of The Great Spirit: bringing him to the world of his native people. His gift to David: a way to finally reconcile what seemed irreconcilable. His very existence.

The entire process took all of two months. The series of ceremonies were allowed by prison officials in the prison yard, on a designated day and time, for sake of them being religious ceremonies that the system needed to accommodate. David eagerly absorbed the nomenclature and behaviors he observed on his spiritual quest. He even pondered the possibility that his life-long illiteracy was evidence that his Native American calling was destined, since all traditions were oral and ritual in nature. As a symbol of devotion and gratitude for having come home to his natural origins he decided to add one more tattoo to his collection: a Native American pattern that was particularly to his liking. With nowhere suitable, or available, amongst his American Mongrel tattoos, he had it applied to his neck, for all to see. Old Joe seemed indifferent to it. "Matters of the flesh do not concern me."

* * *

"You are ready to meet The Great Spirit now. The ceremony that will bring you to him is forbidden by the white men: their prison won't allow the ceremony to take place on its grounds. So we will need to travel three hours by prison bus to Pawhuska, Oklahoma, on the Osage Reservation where we will conduct the ceremony."

Upon arrival Old Joe, David and four other prisoners were unshackled and led off the bus to a large tepee. Osage Indian men were tall—all well over six feet—square shouldered and a handsome people with rugged, balanced and chiseled features: lantern jaw, well-proportioned straight nose, and masculine brow line. Women were barred from any of the ceremonies and understandably kept at a distance from David and the other prisoners, but from what he could see they looked like the men—only shorter and rounder edged.

On the prison bus, Old Joe had explained that none of the Osage would be participating in the ritual. "They do not believe in our ways, the sacrament of the Native American Church, but are a generous people and let us use their lands for our ceremony because otherwise we would have no place to go."

David admired the Osage's tolerance but had no idea what such a sacrament was, or why it might be objectionable—to them or the federal prison system. There was still so much for him to learn, but he knew he would find out soon enough.

Entering the tepee David found a half-moon shaped earthen mound built around a fire that was being attended to by the impending ceremony's chief. Beside him on the ground was neatly organized ceremonial paraphernalia, some covered by a small woven cloth. David was told to make himself comfortable since the ceremony would last all night and conclude with a communion breakfast.

"We join here in brotherly love," the chief began. "Here, in this now sacred place seeking guidance from Wakan Tanka, who kindly offers us his wisdom and spiritual power. To give our eyes the power to see through *his* vision, so that we may see what he sees; that which is now unseen to us. To commune with him and those who now reside in the spiritual world."

The ceremonial chief began by sending a message to Wakan Tanka, to alert him that they were on their way, and he began chanting and singing accompanied by Old Joe and an older prisoner among them who spoke the language. The others, like David, sat quietly, respectfully absorbing the trappings of the ceremony. Taken from a re-purposed mason jar amongst his paraphernalia, the chief sprinkled what looked like dried herbs into the fire, created bluish smoke that symbolized the spirit of the Thunderbird rising up to bring their prayers to Wakan Tanka. This was followed by a sprinkling of water from a sacred river into the fire to send the white smoke of the Waterbird spirit to do the same.

Over the next two hours David watched the chief and Old Joe go though a series of rituals with the seriousness and deliberateness of courtroom legal procedures. It was sunset when their focus shifted from the ceremony to the participants.

The chief pulled back the woven cloth revealing a wooden bowl filled with fleshy green dumpling-shaped bulbs. He donned rubber gloves, cut a small slice from one of them, mashed it in a mortar and pestle, scraped the resulting paste into a tea ball, and infused a mug filled with hot water with it. He made the same preparation for each person in the room one-by-one, appearing to adjust the amount slightly to accommodate for the size of each person.

It was peyote.

David had taken this hallucinogen before, but in its mescaline form: one of the many illegal drugs that the American Mongrels had traded in.

"Brother David," Old Joe turned, handing him his mug. "It is time to allow the divine messenger, peyote, our sacrament, to take you to Wakan Tanka."

David did not take the mug from Old Joe's hands.

Old Joe was taken aback by David's rejection. "He gave it to us for this purpose—to join with him," he implored. "It is his gift to us. We say peyote is the flesh of God."

David still didn't take it. He knew enough that to get up and walk out of the tepee and break the ceremonial circle that he was now a part of would be an affront. Rather, he patiently sat through the entire ceremony until dawn the next day, observing each of the other participants retreat into their personal psychedelic experience. It wasn't the first time he'd been the designated driver.

But David was emotionally distraught now, anguished that he'd been led down another dead end on his search for his Savior. If his Savior had visited him 60-days sober in a Guaynabo Puerto Rico Federal Prison solitary cell and saved him from the brink of hell, he certainly wouldn't find him in drug-induced hallucinations.

* * *

David genuinely appreciated the time, effort and sincerity that Old Joe had invested in him. He could sense that Old Joe, too, was crushed—by his disappointment in David. Old Joe's silence toward him during the communal breakfast and the ride back to prison indicated as much. He felt he owed Old Joe an explanation, but out of respect would not impose it upon him. Rather, he would either wait until Old Joe asked, or simply let it go unsaid. As it turned out, Old Joe never spoke with David again during his stay at FCL El Rino. Perhaps Old Joe already knew the reason why.

CHAPTER 7

Federal Detention Center–Miami was notorious for its heat and humidity during the summer months. FCL El Rino may have gotten hotter in numbers, but owing to the higher humidity the perceived temperature at David's next prison in Miami was indeed worse. During the summer months, prisoners would be allowed outside only early morning and after the late afternoon's 15-minute deluge that would appear like clockwork every day to cool things down to bearable. It wasn't until the Fall, though, that he could stake out a private spot in the yard aside the first inner fence for the better part of the day to escape the drab grey of the prison.

Looking up at the most beautifully blue sky he'd ever seen, through shimmering razor wire strung atop the chain link fence beside him, he heard a voice—it was faint at first, almost inaudible. Struggling to listen, he thought it told him to write something down. He paid it no mind, though, and returned to admiring the extreme color contrasts of the region: the intense green of the local flora, under the cobalt blue sky that most of the time was decorated with the whitest, most heavenly-looking clouds imaginable.

Prepare to write something down.

David was stricken with urgency and leapt to his feet when the voice came through again, but this time loud and clear. "But I can't write," he said aloud, bearing once again the shame of his illiteracy.

Several nearby prisoners looked blankly at David, not sure what to make of his behavior. All except *Smokey*, the old black chain-smoking prisoner who was a fixture in FDC-Miami: he only laughed while overtly nodding his head. Every prison David had been to had an old lifer like Smokey—in one form or another. Ask anyone and they'd tell you he'd been there and would be there forever. FDC-Miami's *Smokey* was probably all of 5 foot, 8 inches tall when he could stand up straight, and his most striking characteristic was his head and neck that strained through the neck hole of his orange prison t-shirt like a tortoise biting for foliage that was just out of reach. Prisoners like Smokey could be paroled if they put in a request, but both prisoner and jailer alike knew that parole at his age and condition would be an act of cruelty. Released with no family to take care of him, his prospects on the outside were most likely a year suffering to death on the streets before being found dead under a bridge somewhere.

Prepare to write something down.

The increasing volume of the voice boiled David's frustration like a pressure cooker in his chest. He clenched his fists, flexed every muscle in his body until he stood there, veins popping, shaking, looking up through the razor wire at the blue sky and this time shouted back: "I can't write!"

Now, in addition to a number of prisoners, several guards had taken notice of David's unusual behavior.

Prepare to write something down!

And that was it for David. He turned and ran across the prison yard at full speed, burst through the doors that led into his cellblock, made a beeline for his cell where he found his cellie lounging. David stood in the cell's doorway out of breath.

"What the hell, Welsh," his cellie demanded, after looking up from his book.

"I just need a pencil and paper. That's all."

"Uh, yeah, sure. There's some in the cigar box on my…"

David was there and gone in a second. "I'll get you more," he said as he burst out of his cell.

David had now become the prison's spectacle of the day, both in the cellblock and the yard as he ran back to his spot by the fence. There, he wrote the first thing he'd written in his adult life:

> I look up to the sky, so beautiful and blue,

and know that what God has created is love so true.

And then in front of my face: razor wire.

I think to myself: what a disgrace,

to know I'm here, the mistakes that I made,

now to rehabilitate myself,

and ask God to take my anger away.

I always found it easy to be evil,

hard to be good,

but now in my life I need God to do the things that I should.

In the ensuing hours of his divine-inspired poetic confession to God his fellow prisoners and guards alike took to calling him Loco Welsh—he could hear it in whispers around him. But he didn't care. The Holy Spirit was still with him and that is all that mattered to him. His quest to find the One who had saved him from hell was renewed. David could feel that he was closer to Him now that he'd made his confession—a personal relationship had begun. He understood that The Holy Spirit was a dimension of God, and he now knew that there was another dimension, a third one, that was still a stranger to him.

And he longed to meet and be in Him the way The Holy Spirit was now in himself.

David ate alone at a table in the prison canteen that evening. The rest of the prisoners carried on around him, but steered clear for whatever was going on with him. It wasn't unusual for an inmate to have a psychotic break, and no one wanted to risk having the handle end of a plastic spoon stabbed into their eye by a fellow prisoner who'd lost it.

The only one who dared approach was Smokey, who waited for David to look up when he arrived at his table. He smiled at David, flashing his mostly toothless grin. "You're talking with the Lord now, huh?" David's heart stopped as Smokey's cataract-fogged eyes seemed to look into his soul. "Well, here, boy," placing a well-read bible on the table. "If you're going to talk with Him, you're going to need to know who He is and what He's already done for you."

CHAPTER 8

22 September, 2006

"Welsh," the prison guard barked through David's cell bars. "Time to move again: back to Atlanta. But the good news? It's from maximum to medium security."

Within ten days he was moved once again, but within the Atlanta system from medium to minimum. And after a week in minimum he was called into a case hearing where David wasn't either behind bars or glass, or chained to the floor in the presence of civilians for the first time in 15 years.

"There was an anomaly with your incarceration," began one of the hearing's officials of a title and federal government agency that David couldn't remember, nor cared to. "We understand that while you were in Guaynabo Puerto Rico Federal Prison you were in solitary confinement for 60 consecutive days."

David sat numb in response to what he was being told. He had been in a dozen case hearings over the years, but he knew they were always just going through the motions. They had no intention of allowing him back into society. And for good reason.

Another official, a lawyerly-looking woman who appeared to be in her 60s, spoke next: "It is unlawful to incarcerate a prisoner in solitary confinement for periods in excess of 15 days in the US federal prison system."

David now focused intently on what was being said.

"Your rights have been violated, Mr. Welsh."

David sat dumbstruck while the various officials in attendance shot looks and glances amongst themselves, at least one of whom was FBI.

FBI Agent Barclay was in his early 50s: a greyed redhead whose reddish speckled skin betrayed years of sun exposure. He wore cliché amber aviator glasses and his equally sun-damaged forearms each bore a tattoo—their identity obscured owing to their having blurred beyond easy recognition over the years. David guessed they were most likely military in origin. He glowered at David: clearly not a supporter of what was about to happen with his case.

"There are two remedies that are on offer to you today, Mr. Welsh," the lawyerly woman went on. "You may remain in this facility while you proceed with a legal process of some complexity—and legal council will be provided..." she said as she searched for, then gestured toward the court-appointed attorney in the room, who smiled and nodded at David. "…or you may wave that process altogether and accept immediate parole under the terms and supervision of the FBI."

* * *

While being measured for civilian clothes, David learned that his shoulder width had decreased by two inches and his waistline had increased by four inches since the day he entered prison 15 years earlier. The possessions he'd entered with were long lost—likely during one of his many moves. His new clothes and a pocket full of twenties that summed to $100 were the only things he had on his person when he was dropped at a city bus stop in the notorious *The Bluff* district—Atlanta's 1.5 square mile dilapidated heroin superstore and shooting gallery. The boarded up and burned out landscape across The Bluff was as much a prison for its inmates as any of the prisons that David had ever passed through. Its prison guards, however, were drug dealers, its bars that locked them in syringes filled with heroin, but the very same gangs who ran Atlanta's prisons also ran The Bluff's streets. The only other difference with prison was The Bluff amounted to one entire death row filled with the condemned. Like so many other parolees, David had been thrown out of one prison only to be dumped into another.

Sitting on a bench inhaling the diesel exhaust from the busses, he pondered his *persona non grata* status. He couldn't vote. He couldn't own a firearm. He couldn't teach in a school, nor hold a professional license. And though a senior officer of the American Mongrels—an organization he helped run that was as complex and requiring as much management and leadership skills as any legitimate business—he couldn't be a supervisor, executive or director in a company that required any fiduciary responsibility. His future was set: he was at that moment all that he was ever going to be, no more. Doing 15 years of a 25-year sentence was akin to entering a time warp. There he was, standing on the same streets of Atlanta but 15 years older, with no other memories to account for the time than the image of the inside of prison walls. Time truly lost.

"You'll be back," he replayed the parting words of FBI Agent Barclay when they met one-on-one the day before his release. "I heard you got Jesus while in prison."

David knew the moment Agent Barclay's scorn and disgust-filled stare bored into him at the hearing, that his acceptance would be elusive.

"I've seen plenty of cell-block conversions. They're a dime a dozen: nothing but a trick, to get lenient treatment from gullible do-gooder parole committees." Agent Barclay had already made up his mind about David, and it would take heaven and earth to change it.

“I just hate the idea that good people will have to be hurt by you again before we can put you back inside a cage.” FBI Agent Barclay’s bitter contempt for David pounded down upon him until he felt as if he were looking up at him from flat on his back in the grave. He chose to remain silent.

Agent Barclay was assigned to David, not so much as a parole officer but to keep track of him, to let him know that he was being watched and to acquire information on any of David’s associates to assist with other on-going investigations. Or start new ones.

“The running bet is 4-to-1 against you: that you’ll be back in within your first four months. I’m betting against you. You personify the recidivist convict, Welsh.”

In spite of it all, David bore no animosity toward Agent Barclay for his cynicism about his prospects: he had no evidence or reason to think differently about him. David would be free, but under FBI surveillance for at least the next ten years—maybe for the rest of his life. David gladly added the weight of Agent Barclay’s doubt and distrust of him to the cross he now bore with every step he took on his mission. David had made his choice: he would not allow Agent Barclay’s judgment and suspicion to trip him up and justify a return to a life of crime. The only life he’d ever known on the outside. Rather, he would embrace their sting as a goad, to keep him moving forward in his new life in service to the Almighty.

The chill of the late autumn air soon set David to walking sidewalks. Under the blank stares of young men sitting on rotten wooden porches in front of a brick and plywood façade of a crumbling building, two police cars and an EMS vehicle were stopped. Their first responders were bringing a body out of a new, four-door Mercedes.

"Robbery-murder?" David asked one of the officers who was standing watch over the scene, protecting his fellow officer and the EMS crew from the The Bluffs' inmates—same as prison guards did for their fellow officers in prison.

"Nope. Overdose. Or bad junk. Same thing, really. It's all poison anyway."

The body that EMS was strapping to the gurney was that of a late teen wearing designer clothes and expensive shoes. "Another silver-spooner," the EMS tech announced to whoever cared to listen.

The policeman looked David over: middle-aged man, wool cap, grey handle bar moustache and dressed for the weather with none of his gang tattoos showing. "Yep. We get two or three of these a week down here," he confided in David. "Silver-spoon junkies. Rich kids from the suburbs coming down here to The Bluffs to buy their heroin, bringing their own syringes, alcohol swabs and a fantasy of invincibility…and eventually this is what you get."

"It's a death sentence being executed," David let out.

The policeman nodded, looking David in the eye. "Somebody's kid." He shook his head.

It felt odd for David to be spoken to like a regular person by a cop. Even before his most recent incarceration, he wasn't able to have a normal conversation of any kind with them. To be fair, in the past, he would only interact with them either while being arrested or during a traffic stop. Still, it felt good to be treated in this way: trusted and being given the benefit of the doubt by someone in a position of authority. He could get used to it.

David knew that while there may have been two or three silver-spooner ODs a week, there were many more who lived in The Bluffs, who were routinely poisoning themselves to death. But they didn't die in a Mercedes. Some didn't even have a broken-down hovel to die in. And still others only had the bare ground, with a roadway bridge as a blanket to pull over themselves for protection and warmth, and to keep out of the rain.

David's rambling brought him under a series of overpasses where the darkness revealed flickering silhouettes that were projected from a fire against a bridge abutment buried deep within the massive interchange's tangles. He jogged across the road, up a slope and over an embankment until the full extent of a make-shift camp was revealed before him. The colorless moonlight painted a black n' white scene right out of a 1930s hobo town—save the orange flames reaching up from within a 50-gallon drum to desperately grab at the night air. There were differences with a 20th-century hobo town. Billed flat caps were replaced by hoodies, patched n' frayed wool jackets with duct-tape patched dirty down coats, and wood alcohol with heroin or any other drug that happened to be available. But there were other similarities. An abandoned and partially stripped vehicle, old tires stacked as chairs, and other broken and discarded items that served as furnishings under several tarp lean-tos. The gaunt and drawn unshaven faces and hollow expressionless eyes of the men who turned to look at David were most certainly the same: hopeless.

Two of the men slowly turned away, back toward the fire, and simultaneously slid apart making room for David on a makeshift bench they'd built out of old wooden pallets. It was as though they were saving a seat for him. Expecting him. FBI Agent Barclay certainly expected him to end up there under the bridges; to join society's other jetsam. So, too, the prison system itself: "About half of all ex-offenders end up returning to prison," the transition counselor coldly read from a pamphlet to David and 3 others whose release was imminent. "The other half? You have a 13 times higher chance of dying your first few weeks out of prison than the general population. A lot are from overdoses from ex-cons who attempt to get high after losing their tolerance for their drug of choice while in prison. Some are murders from settling old scores. A fair number are from suicide…" And then there were his father's words that rankled in his subconscious, only bubbling up to his consciousness on occasions when he needed reminding: "Garbage always makes its way into the gutter eventually," he would sometimes grumble when David, the child would disobey or cause trouble while rebelling against authority.

Hopelessness.

David pondered the seat that awaited him before the 21st-century hobo camp fire—convinced that he was at a turning point. He could turn away now, or spend the rest of his life under the bridges of Atlanta.

David turned away, returning to the road and retracing the way he'd come.

* * *

The under-bridgeway camp had added a few more derelicts to their number by the time David returned with a large duffel bag slung over his shoulder and carrying a cardboard case marked: Meals Ready To Eat (MRE). He had only 32 cents now in his pocket, having spent the rest of his $100 at a military surplus store that he'd passed on the way from the bus stop. From the duffel bag he withdrew and distributed tightly rolled wool blankets, followed by a box of three folded emergency one-time use disposable stoves, a jar of instant coffee, a camper's coffee pot, plastic disposable cups, 16 half-liters of bottled water, a ten-pack of wool glove liners without their gloves, an eight pack of Ivory soap bars, a bag of disposable tooth brushes individually wrapped together with a tiny tube of toothpaste, and a six-pack of toilet paper.

Though David knew there was hunger in the camp (he could smell it, having himself lived hungry and cowered outdoors in his youth), the men remained dignified and well-mannered—each calmly taking their turns selecting an MRE from its case until it was empty. The men ate in silence, the warmth of a fresh hot meal perhaps helping them retreat into their own world of personal memories. Childhood memories of dinners with their parents and siblings, David imagined. Or meals with their own families before addiction and criminality shattered both their families and lives and landed them under the bridges.

"What's your name, friend?" one of the men asked; he was the last of the hobos to wrap himself in a blanket before heading up under one of the bridges to find a place to sleep off his meal in one of the cubbyholes created where the bridge's main girder beams met its concrete abutment.

Time of course wasn't the only thing that David had left in prison. He'd also left his earthly identity there. David Welsh was a mere shadow now, someone who was put in prison a decade and a half earlier. And that is where David Welsh would remain: in prison. There was only one thing in his life that wasn't corrupted, that was pure: his passion for the word of God and spreading it. "Teach them what I taught you and love them the way I love you:" God's words that had brought him back to the hobo camp. And he heard the man ask again: "What is your name, friend?"

"Call me Pastor 7."

* * *

After receiving the bible from Smokey many months earlier, David returned to his cell and began reading. He would read Genesis straight through to Revelation in fewer than three months. From the first word of the first sentence on the first page, the writing became words, and words became sentences: for the first time in his life he began to read. And he knew it was God who had removed the source of his greatest humiliation—his illiteracy—from him, which he now understood was in and of itself a gift. Having never received formal education, never been trained in one channel of thinking, no fixed process nor approach to problem solving impressed upon him in a school, he was forced to exercise his mind and power of reason to a broader extent than most educated people. His lack of formal education forced the necessity of finding unconventional and novel ways to arrive at understanding and devise solutions. Street smarts. It was how he perceived the world and he was now applying it to understanding the bible. And so he consumed each and every word, held each in his mouth, first savoring their unique individual flavor, then the melody of flavors together with the words around it and ultimately the idea that emerged from blending them all—with complete understanding. He would then greedily pick up the next word and do the same, for his thirst for these words was truly insatiable. And it was in this way that God's gift of his life-long illiteracy now served him. No one who'd read books their entire life could have wanted to read this book more than he.

The Holy Spirit had come to him and never left him, and the Old Testament brought him to the God of Abraham, but these were not the facet of God who had pulled him back from hell in that Guaynabo solitary cell.

It wasn't until he reached the New Testament, and the books of Matthew, Mark, Luke, John, that he finally met his Savior at his epiphany: at John 14:6. He read out loud:

> "I am the way and the truth and the life.
>
> No one comes to the Father except through me."

David Welsh fell to his knees as he'd done before and this time declared aloud:

> "I believe in God the Father,
>
> I believe in The Holy Spirit,
>
> I believe in Jesus Christ,
>
> I believe in the crucifixion,

I believe Jesus conquered
death,

I believe He has transformed
my life."

Tears rolled down his cheeks: "My Lord, my Savior, I have finally found you."

CHAPTER 9

Though he was broke and keeping company of hobos under one of Atlanta's bridges his first night a free man, it was not Pastor 7's destiny to remain under them more than one night. Wandering far the next morning, Pastor 7 happened upon a furniture store owner who was standing alone behind her store smoking a cigarette. She presented a frail silhouette, burdened by some great weight on her shoulders, he thought as he cautiously approached so as not to frighten her—they were on the edge of The Bluff after all. He could discern from the 1,000-yard stare she wore upon her low-slung leathery face that she was indeed bearing some kind of burden.

"What's troubling you, dear?"

She squinted at Pastor 7, trying to bring into focus who he was and what he might have wanted from her. She was finely coiffured, for the present neighborhood anyway: her hair appeared professionally done, her overcoat fine wool or cashmere, and her hands and nails manicured. She was wise enough to not wear jewelry—but it didn't take a stretch of the imagination to believe that she may have had a respectable collection of it at home. Satisfied that he wasn't a threat she offered him a cigarette.

In the space of three chain-smoked cigarettes she explained that her husband of 35 years had recently died and left her the furniture business on the brink of failure. Once a thriving business, spill-over crime from neighboring The Bluff had driven the value, quality and safety of the area down to a point where customers simply went elsewhere—so selling the business wasn't an option. "Nobody wanted it," she said through a hurried exhale of smoke, clearly having surrendered to her fate. Her only option was a going-out-of-business sale and to walk away.

In spite of her circumstances she was not seeking anyone's pity. She told her story dispassionately and her body language supported her tough and unflappable demeanor. But her eyes could not hide her desperation when she explained that she and her husband never had children and that she was now alone in the world. Alone, unneeded, unwanted. "It's just the way things are, that's all. If I'd died before my husband he'd be the one taking care of everything alone."

The mid-day sun had warmed the air and she opened the top buttons of her overcoat, revealing a cross around her neck.

"You already know that someone always wants you and loves you," Pastor 7 said, making a point of letting her know that he was able to see her cross. “Let’s pray.” Pastor 7 offered his hands palms up. She placed her frail, slightly trembling, smoke-stained fingers into his powerful hands that grasped them gently. “What’s your name dear?”

“Gale,” she said meekly in her smoker’s voice.

There, together behind her store, Pastor 7 led the prayer for Gale, who afterward commented that it was one of the most gracious and beautifully spoken prayers she’d ever heard. She quizzically gazed into his eyes: “What are *you* doing here?”

“God told me to go under the bridges and set His captives free.”

She invited him in for coffee.

* * *

When Gale saw Pastor 7 drive up in her store’s delivery truck six weeks after they’d met she dropped her cigarette and rubbed it out with the toe of her shoe, then unlocked the padlock to the warehouse door at the back of her store. David was returning from the food bank.

Gale was now a revitalized woman: vibrant and energetic, she moved with a sense of purpose in her step. Pastor 7 hopped down from the delivery truck’s cab: “Tell the men its time to work for their supper and help me unload this…” he said to her. But Gale didn’t need to tell them. Rather, she stood smiling proudly with her arms confidently crossed as the warehouse door rolled open behind her and eight men appeared from within the warehouse to unload the two pallets and a large ice chest from the back of the truck. Atop the pallets, an eclectic mix of packaged snack foods cases: Snickers bars, Sun Chips, beef jerky, Ritz Crackers, and Granola bars, among others. And, two-dozen loaves of bread and as many 12-packs of shrink-wrapped half-liter bottles of water. In the cooler on ice: packaged bologna and ham, assorted Lunchables and sliced process cheese.

Once unloaded, the goods entered a production line set up in the warehouse beside the nine beds that Gale had provided for the men, and Pastor 7. One of the men had worked in the restaurant business and ensured everyone followed ServeSafe-certified practices as they made sandwiches, wrapped them in plastic wrap, added them to individual plastic bags that had been stuffed with a single bottle of water and a couple of handfuls of the snack foods. Each was placed in large garbage bags that at dusk made their way into the back of an ancient 11-seat Ford Econoline van that had recently been donated to Pastor 7 and Gale for the purpose.

Though Pastor 7 was a consummate organizer and leader, he happily let Gale run the show. After opening her warehouse to the homeless she had transformed into a new vivacious version of herself. She had meaning in her life again and, running things on her feet, she was clearly back in her element. She looked and moved like someone 20 years her younger. Days began at 5:30 am with the hygiene regimen. 6:00 am: bible study. 7:00 am: breakfast. All the men were handy and skilled in one trade or another and they spent the early part of the day fixing up Gale's store. It worked: the store's improved appearance picked up business enough to keep income just ahead of expenses.

In the van on the way to and from the home improvement store, the bible study continued. Lunch: over more bible study. And in the afternoon, Pastor 7 would assume the role of teaching pastor for an hour or two—a skill he'd perfected in prison, where all the men in his discipleship program had been before. After the food bags were packed, at sunset, the discipleship spilled out of the warehouse onto the streets of Atlanta with the crew piling into the Econoline and fanning out under the bridges. The men in Pastor 7's discipleship knew the street because they'd come from it, literally. Pastor 7 had rescued them from under the bridges and into Gale's warehouse. Their connection was strong with those they found still existing there. They met them, hugged them and gave each of them a meal. And the opportunity to join in an impromptu group prayer on the spot—if they wanted to.

Pastor 7 discovered that the most heart-felt street prayers always seemed to come spontaneously and from the most unexpected of the under-bridge dwellers. Invariably, from any one of the ragged anonymous caricatures joining hands would come a powerful voice, charismatically reciting a prayer as eloquently composed and well-spoken as any from the pulpit of a church. And another would lead them in song, a hymn familiar to all, inspiring those present with a voice that was so melodic and powerful that even the non-believers in the vicinity couldn't help but be raised up by it. The unexpected sources of such prayers and song were not only evidence to Pastor 7 of God's grace, they brought home the depth of the tragedy of these people losing their lives to addiction and despair: that all of these caricatures huddled in blankets around campfires were once individuals, people who'd had identities, families and lives within the greater civilization before they fell far, under the bridges.

And this is what Pastor 7 did every day, all day, from the day he was released from prison: going under the bridges and setting His captives free.

* * *

From time to time Pastor 7 would see Agent Barclay in a sedan across the street watching the activity at Gale's store. Apparently, six months after Pastor 7's release from prison, Agent Barclay's suspicions became irresistible and Pastor 7 became David Welsh again: handcuffed and lying face down on the warehouse floor—the disconcerting feeling of a boot on the center of his back. Men and women with FBI emblazoned upon their backs swarmed the warehouse and, now, three donated Econoline vans parked outside: one with a cross within angel wings and

"7 Bridges To Recovery" painted on its side. The agents dug through and emptied the three well-used commercial refrigerator / freezers that had been donated by a local restaurant owner who went out of business. They tore open cases of packaged food and their contents—Dorito chips, flavored shelled peanuts and other things—piled up on the floor. A folding table-top test lab was set up and used to test everything from sample bottles of water to juice boxes.

And they were likely doing the same at the house that had been donated two months earlier by a family whose mother had passed away in it. Her children lived in various parts of the country, and though she'd owned the house and left it to them, none of her children wanted to deal with it. The house was in a so-so neighborhood and fixing it up for sale would cost as much as what they could get for it. One of the children was devout and she'd read a story about Pastor 7 and Gale's street ministry in her church's newsletter. She convinced her siblings to donate the house and split the tax deduction. After the men had fixed it up it became the residence of 12 of the 20 men Pastor 7 now had under the wings of his street ministry. Pastor 7 only hoped Gale wasn't having to endure a raid at her house.

A drug-sniffing dog was licking Pastor 7's face when a peeved Agent Barclay ordered his handcuffs removed and him picked up off the floor. Though the warehouse was now a mess, David smiled as he looked around. “It’s understandable. This would look pretty bad knowing who I was.”

This must not have been the response that Agent Barclay was expecting from Pastor 7, as his expression transformed from one of exasperation to embarrassment. Forgiveness from a career criminal, convict?

The room was frozen: agents and 7 Bridges To Recovery men alike, awaiting orders. “Yeah. It does.”

“Can our men begin putting things back in the freezers now? Before they spoil?” Pastor 7 asked politely.

Agent Barclay nodded his agreement then led Pastor 7 to an FBI van for interrogation. They spent the next hour going over known associates of David Welsh. From their discussion, Pastor 7 discovered that three of his former American Mongrel members were dead, four others serving life sentences.

“Just because we haven’t been able to document any contact that you’ve had with your associates….”

“Former associates.”

“Associates…but that doesn’t mean anything Welsh. We know how clever you are. We’ve just not been able to figure out what your angle is with this so-called ministry of yours, that’s all.” When Agent Barclay waved over a younger agent who presented

Pastor 7 with a dozen or so photos, Pastor 7 could sense Agent Barclay's mounting desperation.

"I'm sorry. I don't know anything about these people. I know some of them, that's true, but I haven't been in contact with any of them since I went in."

Clearly frustrated, Agent Barclay paused for a moment, scratching the crown of his balding head to think, then appeared to give up. He ordered the van door opened and Pastor 7 let out.

"You realize that being with you like this now, so visible, could get me killed. The Mongrels don't take chances. Neither do some of their former enemies."

"I guess that's just a chance you'll have to take, Welsh" Agent Barclay said, smiling cynically through bad teeth as he rolled the van door shut in Pastor 7's face.

* * *

Pastor 7 lamented being stuck in the chair of the 7 Bridges To Recovery mission's office at The Garden. It was dusk and he knew without looking that the food bags were packed, vans loaded and that volunteers were mounting up to head out under the bridges to distribute food, prayers and uplifting song to the needy. It had been ten years now, and still, from the day he was released from prison, all he'd done since, went toward feeding and ministering under the bridges and setting His captives free. His passion and desire for personally ministering to the last, lost and the least under the bridges was as potent as the day he'd brought blankets, food and water back to the hobo camp. But he had to think about what his accountant had told him earlier that day about the cash-flow issues his ministry was facing that month. Though his 7 Bridges To Recovery ministry was a 501c3, it still needed to pay its bills. But Pastor 7 knew that despair was pointless: his Savior had provided what was needed from the day he stood on that street corner with a new suit of clothes and $100 in his pocket. Today was just another day. 7 Bridges To Recovery had become a well-oiled machine over the previous decade. Through the graces of many benefactors, his vans continued to roll out each evening, now delivering 3,000 meals each week during the peak season.

And when more men sought refuge, recovery and rehabilitation, his ministry was provided another house, and another with which to receive them and bring them into a discipleship program that he had created for them. By the time the fourth house was added, 30 men on any given day would refuge in the mission's houses and have the opportunity to start a new life after addiction, prison and a career of crime. Most of the men would remain within his ministry for a year, the length of his men's discipleship program.

And when the needs of women and children from the streets of Atlanta were brought to him, The Garden was provided: a 100-year-old church and adjoining buildings that were made available for his ministry. Its facilities were repurposed for dormitory housing and a dining hall that accommodated up to 100 residents who sought refuge from the neglect, abuse and drug dens where they were imprisoned. Six out of ten were women, the rest, their children. And it took on average one year too, to resuscitate a soul from certain death on the street back to life and independence.

And then there were The Garden's staff who dedicated their heart and soul to the mission. And those who made pilgrimage to his ministry in order to help, too. Volunteer "mission teams" who came from all over the country, often up to 50 students who gladly gave up a week of their summer vacation, to volunteer and make a difference.

All told, The Garden now provided three meals a day to approximately 130 residents, staff and volunteers 365 days a year. Volunteer professionals would stand by residents in court, when seeking to recover custody of a child that had been taken into Child Protection Services for their safety. They would correspond with probation and parole officers advocating and providing recommendations when a resident had passed the point of no return with their recovery. They received help with reacquiring documents such as birth certificates, photo ID's, driver licenses. Former teachers volunteered to teach GED classes, and still others donated or finance outside GED courses, helping them prepare to earn a high school diploma and improve their employability. And, of course donated cars given away: 25 in the previous seven years to literally get their people back on the road to independence. Everything and anything that was needed to re-start and rebuild their shattered lives.

Pastor 7 sliced open an envelope that bore a return address from the Formosan Christian Church of Dallas that contained a $ 25,000 check, along with a joint letter from the pastors there explaining that the money was pooled by their parishioners. Pastor 7 smiled serenely: this is the way it's happened for ten years now, and with joy and deep gratitude filling his heart, he said aloud: "You always provide."

The cantankerous growl of a Harley Davidson motorcycle's panhead engine arrived, then wound down to its pop, pop…pop, pop…pop, pop gasping idol before gagging to a stop outside his pastor's residence door. No one at the motorcycle club had a panhead. And the FBI certainly wasn't riding them.

As he rose from his chair to see who was at his door, Pastor 7 felt a twinge in his gut and his heart race a little: a long-ago established reflex when facing the unknown. His instinct wasn't an overreaction: he knew the man who he met at his doorway. A man who was contracted to kill David Welsh 25 years earlier.

The man was dressed in full leathers and had aged about as well as David had: their requisite battle-hardened bodies now sporting a modest but requisite paunch above their belt buckles, hung beneath more rounded and less bulky shoulders. Their white facial hair, and wrinkled and mottled faces betrayed the gulf of time between the present and when they'd last met. Nevertheless, Pastor 7 knew that contracts were forever.

"Do you remember me?"

"The face, but not the name."

"Pastor Jake," the man said automatically. Catching himself: "You'd know me as Jake…from the Johnny Rebs motorcycle club."

Pastor 7 was relieved the moment his guest first identified himself as Pastor Jake. He thanked God that he would not need to face the paradox between self-defense and serving the Prince of Peace that day. He invited Pastor Jake in and offered him a seat, but Pastor Jake had another idea: he reached out and embraced Pastor 7 in a bear hug and began to cry. "Thank you for not killing me," Pastor Jake blurted.

David Welsh had found out about Jake having accepted the contract to take his life a quarter-century ago. David then staked out Jake for nearly a week before he could get him alone behind an Atlanta strip club where Jake had gone to discretely snort cocaine. David got his attention by placing the business end of his trademark custom Colt 1911 45 against Jake's forehead.

"If I ever see you again, you're dead," David threatened, pressing the barrel hard against Jake's forehead. "Hell, I might just kill you now to be sure,"

Pastor 7 remembered Jake standing strong as he reached into his belt and pockets and took his sidearm, knife and brass knuckles. He then pistol-whipped Jake with his own pistol and proceeded to artfully apply his skills surgically bruising, battering and breaking the human body. Now semiconscious in a heap next to the strip club's dumpster, David could have just as easily gutted him with Jake's knife, or plunged it into the top of his skull as a message for anyone else who might consider taking up the contract on his life. But for some reason he didn't. Something about Jake's taking his beating without a whimper or pleading—as David had the last night his father beat him—brought a sense of respect and mercy to David's heart that night.

"I'm so sorry for what I did to you," Pastor 7 apologized to the fellow repentant man in his arms.

The men pulled away and collected themselves. Having regained their composure they drank coffee and talked until the early hours about their ministries and lives since their rebirth. Pastor Jake had served time too, though not as much as Pastor 7 had. Both had already "lived their's" and were now living for the Almighty and the people they served. Pastor Jake led a respectable bikers' street ministry in St. Louis, where reborn bikers from any club would ride together wearing the colors of Christ. They agreed that their clubs would ride to the other's cities and join in each other's street ministries on special occasions each year: Easter, Independence Day, Thanksgiving, and weather permitting, Christmas.

Pastor 7 offered him to stay in one of the ministry's houses as long as he liked, but Pastor Jake was already checked into a nearby hotel and planned to leave the next morning. Pastor 7 walked him out to his panhead that had been restored to perfection. Pastor Jake mounted his steed, kicked it to life and tapped it into first gear. "Thanks for the hospitality, 7."

Both men stared at each other, and save the grumblings of the vintage motorcycle, silently contemplated the power of God in their lives through their reflections in the other—neither of them having to share their survivor's guilt when it came to thinking about the other battle-scarred gladiators who were unable to escape death in the arena: their former lives. It was understood.

"Hey, I'm glad you didn't kill me either."

CHAPTER 10

"It was Agent Barclay, wasn't it?" Pastor 7 asked Deputy Pardon Attorney Sarah Abraham as he watched her feverishly type into her laptop.

"Yes." She smiled, not looking up. Sensing the weight of Pastor 7's silence, she stopped typing and looked at him: "He was the one who recommended you for Presidential Pardon."

A year after Agent Barclay's attempted bust at Gale's furniture store, a city urban renewal project bought her land at a good price, providing her a comfortable retirement. After that, Pastor 7 had seen Agent Barclay or other FBI agents surveilling him from time to time: on the road with his motorcycle club, under bridges while handing out food and prayers, and while monitoring the goings on at The Garden from afar. But Agent Barclay's plans to use him to inform on people who he no longer associated with failed. For the FBI, David Welsh had become a dead end.

Pastor 7 recalled receiving Agent Barclay's final visit at The Garden's pastor's residence: the first time he'd ever set foot inside. He looked all of a tired old man who was finished with his career and was gliding to retirement within weeks. He'd lost most of his hair years earlier, but unlike David, he still carried on the battle with comb-overs and hair spray. "I was wrong about you, David," he said while looking at his feet. "I've never seen a more total and sincere conversion of a man in my entire 40-year career," he said in a near apologetic tone.

"There are many more of us who've reformed. I see it every day within our men's discipleship program."

"I'm sure there are. But you? You are an exception in all respects. You? I'm absolutely certain that you've given your life to this," he said while looking at the church through a window.

Pastor 7 only nodded.

"My recommendation will be that your case be closed. You won't be seeing us anymore."

Pastor 7 was relieved, but waited for the catch. "I'll miss having you guys around," he said with a wry smile. "Your surveillance keeps the burglars away."

Agent Barclay put his hand on his hips, "David…" He drew, then released a long breath. "That's only the FBI case. You are still on the hook with the Justice Department. Your remaining ten years is still in force if Justice feels you've violated the terms of your parole."

"I understand."

Agent Barclay turned and looked Pastor 7 directly in the eyes. "I can't do anything about that. Only a presidential pardon could change that."

"I understand." Pastor 7 could see that Agent Barclay was genuinely distraught about his legal circumstances. "I appreciate all you are doing."

Pastor 7's forgiving tone appeared to put Agent Barclay a little more at ease. "That is unless you decided to rob a bank," he chuckled, smiling kindly.

* * *

Deputy Pardon Attorney Abraham powered-off her laptop, stood in Pastor 7's office and sent him a warm, genuine smile over his desk. "I think we're done here, Mr. Welsh. We'll keep you informed as to the status of your application."

CHAPTER 11

When news got around The Garden that Pastor 7 would receive a Presidential Pardon and would go to Washington D.C. and the White House to personally receive it from the President, two residents marched up to his office ordered him to his feet and began taking measurements from head to toe. The women had been seamstresses most of their lives—before alcoholism, spousal abandonment and their jobs moving overseas pushed them into the ranks of the homeless.

"What's this all about?" Pastor 7 asked as they instructed him to raise his arms while taking measurements.

"Shut up," one said. "It's a surprise, don't spoil it," said the other.

The day he was leaving for the airport, Pastor 7 put on the first suit he'd worn since his appearance at his last sentencing: receiving 25 years to life for the privilege. He nearly cried when he read the hand-embroidered inscription that the ladies had sewn along the rim of the jacket's inside pocket: "David Welsh." He finally did tear up when the seamstresses led him to

The Garden's packed dining hall, and to cheers as he was presented a cake with the lettering: "Welcome Home David Welsh," beside the image of a yellow ribbon wrapped around a tree.

Five days later, in a taxi on his way to Ronald Reagan Washington National Airport to fly back to Atlanta, David Welsh reread a letter written on plain paper bearing the seal of the Department of Justice:

Executive Grant of Clemency

President of the United States of America.

To all to whom these presents shall come, greeting:

Be it known, that this day the President has granted unto David Adam Welsh

A full and unconditional pardon

For his crimes against persons, property, and society, last of which resulting in his conviction and sentencing to life in prison of not less than 25 years and his subsequent incarceration and parole from thereof

The President has designated, directed and empowered the Pardon Attorney to act as his representative to sign this grant of executive clemency.

In accordance with these instructions and authority I have signed my name and caused the seal of the Department of Justice to be affixed below and affirm that this action is the act of the President being performed at his direction.

Done at the city of Washington, District of Columbia

By the direction of the President

Beneath the signature of the Pardon Attorney appeared a date that was not lost to David: it was 25 years to the month from his last conviction. David Welsh had served his entire sentence. And not only was he now a completely free man, all his convictions were null and void. He could vote. He could own a firearm, if he chose. He could teach in a school and earn a professional license. And could hold fiduciary responsibility in a position of executive authority: such as his own 7 Bridges To Recovery 501c3, which up to now had to be done through surrogates. He was not just free, he was reinstated to what he was before he was sent to his first adult prison. His heart soared at the realization that he was again reborn: he had regained his earthly identity. Looking out the window of the taxi he saw the dome of the Jefferson Memorial and recited in a whisper the most inspiring inscription there:

"We hold these truths to be self-evident,
that all men are created equal,

that they are endowed by their Creator with certain unalienable Rights,

that among these are Life, Liberty and the pursuit of Happiness.

That to secure these rights Governments are instituted among men,

deriving their just powers from the consent of the governed..."

David marveled at the irony that the American government, which was created for the sole purpose of guaranteeing God-given rights, had now seen fit to redeem him—same as his Savior had. Redeemed in the eyes of his Savior, he was now redeemed in the eyes of his country and so his country had lived up to the promise of its founding.

David's cell phone buzzed in his pocket. It was a message from his sister, the only family member he'd ever kept in touch with. She never visited him while he was in prison but every Christmas, whatever prison he was in, she'd always sent him a Christmas card. They met a couple of times after he was released, but owing to her living in California they mostly kept in touch by e-mail and texts. The joy in David's heart about his legal emancipation was compounded by his appreciation for his sister having taken the time to keep up with developments in his life and think of him on this day—one of the greatest days of his life. Her message read:

Dad is dying   stroke   you're
there   he's in Walter Reed
medical   can't get away now
can you represent us siblings

After indulging himself with a moment of reflection and the Almighty with a prayer he instructed the taxi driver to take him to Walter Reed Military Medical Center.

* * *

So this is where it all ended for Adam Welsh: alone, in a hospital bed hooked up to a ventilator and IVs waiting for death to take him. Through wars, beatings, frostbite, nearly a year in a POW camp, malnutrition, infections, numerous surgeries, smoking and drinking, and a bitter marriage that culminated in a failed family life, his gristly old man hung in there for 91 years. As David stood quietly beside his father, pondering him as a person, the life he'd led and the demons who'd haunted him, the thought arose that people's faces at his father's age—having lost subcutaneous fat and elasticity in their skin sunken against underlying bone—meant all of us ended up looking pretty much the same at the end. The last time he'd seen his father was the day he was moved from the juvenile facility to adult prison. He hadn't even seen a photograph of him. The only distinguishing feature that let David know that this living corpse who lay before him was his father was the outline of the steel plate beneath his scalp.

His father must have sensed his presence there at his bedside and he opened his eyes. He attempted to turn his head to see who was there, but was unable to owing to the ventilator. David accommodated by moving his face into his father's field of vision. His father's eyes showed no sign of recognition.

"It's David, dad. Your son."

Paralyzed on his left side, Adam Welsh reached out to grab his son's forearm with his right hand. His grip was still strong, all things considered. David had dealt with many tortured and helpless souls over the years, even those on the verge of death, but this one was of course different. David grasped his father's hand, closed his eyes and prayed that his father was saved. That the Almighty's redemption had been bestowed upon his everlasting soul.

"Dad, listen to me," he pulled his father's hand to his chest. "In spite of everything in our past, I love you and I forgive you for everything. I love you dad."

A tear rolled down his father's cheek before he slipped back into unconsciousness. He would never wake in this life again. Through his touch and the grace of God, he searched his father's soul for the demons of anger and hate that had consumed both of them and done their best to wreck their lives. They were nowhere to be found. And so was doused the family torch of anger and hate that had been passed down to him so many years earlier.

David thanked the Almighty for the privilege of allowing him to do his part to help redeem the life and soul of Adam Welsh.

The End

Trademarked terms listed in The Last, The Lost, and the Least include:

Harley Davidson™

Road King™

Colt 1911 A1™

Snickers™

Sun Chips™

Ritz Crackers™

Granola™

Lunchables™

ServeSafe™

Econoline™

Dorito™

MRE: Meals Ready to Eat™

For more information on this ministry, contact them at:

7 Bridges to Recovery

2840 Plant Atkinson Road

Atlanta, GA 30339

404-644-6976

7bridgestorecovery@gmail.com

www.7bridgestorecovery.org